Ziggy and the

#2

Black Dinosaurs

Lost in the Tunnel of Time

By Sharon M. Draper

Illustrated by Jesse Joshua Watson

Aladdin Paperbacks
New York London Toronto Sydney

This book is dedicated to
Elijah, Malachi, and Deshawn

❦

ALADDIN PAPERBACKS
An imprint of Simon & Schuster Children's Publishing Division
1230 Avenue of the Americas, New York, NY 10020
Text copyright © 1996, 2006 by Sharon M. Draper
Illustrations copyright © 2006 by Jesse Joshua Watson
All rights reserved, including the right of reproduction
in whole or in part in any form.
ALADDIN PAPERBACKS and colophon are trademarks of
Simon & Schuster, Inc.
Designed by Lisa Vega
The text of this book was set in Minion.
Manufactured in the United States of America
First Aladdin Paperbacks edition 2006
This book, in slightly different format,
was originally published by Just Us Books.
8 10 9
Library of Congress Control Number 2005927491
ISBN-13: 978-0-689-87912-8
ISBN-10: 0-689-87912-1

One

Like cool, sweet milk on a bowl of crunchy cereal, the Thursday morning breeze splashed the crisp, dry leaves under Rico's feet. He liked this time of year. It would soon be time for warm fires in the fireplace and frosty snow on the sidewalk. His mom had made him wear a jacket to school today, and it felt good. As he crossed the street to the school building, he spotted his friend Ziggy and waved.

Ziggy sat on the front steps of the school, digging wildly in his book bag. He pulled out two broken pencils, a half-eaten apple, a red spiral notebook, a sandwich wrapped in plastic, a doorknob, and a green tennis shoe. "Hey, Rico-mon! Did you do your history homework?"

Rico chuckled. "Sure, Ziggy. It was easy. Didn't you do yours?"

"Of course I did it, mon—Ziggy is no fool. But I can't *find* it!"

Ziggy continued to empty the contents of his book bag on the school steps—his math book, seven small smooth rocks, five nickels, and a purple three-ring binder. "It's gotta be in here somewhere," he mumbled to himself. His long braided hair, covered with a small, green and yellow knitted cap, hung over his shoulders.

"What are the rocks for?" asked Rico.

"I call them the Seven Special Stones of the Sun," replied Ziggy mysteriously as he held the rocks in his hand for Rico to see.

"Why do you call them that? What makes them so special?"

"My grandmother gave them to me, mon. She brought them all the way from Jamaica. She told me they would bring me good luck."

"They look like ordinary rocks to me," Rico said with doubt.

"Well, that just shows how much you know, mon," Ziggy said as he rolled the stones in his palm. He looked thoughtful, then asked, "Can you keep a secret, Rico?"

"Sure," replied Rico, who never knew what Ziggy would do or say.

"These stones . . ." Ziggy paused for a moment. He looked around to make sure no one was listening. His voiced dropped to a whisper. "These stones keep away *ghosts*!"

"Ghosts?" Rico laughed nervously. "There are no ghosts around here!"

"See how well the stones are working, mon?" Ziggy replied with glee. Rico laughed again, shaking his head at his friend. Ziggy plopped the stones back into his book bag.

Just then a gust of wind blew through the school-yard and across the steps. The pages of Ziggy's red notebook fluttered and gently released the one sheet of paper that had been tucked inside. Ziggy's large, round handwriting boldly filled both sides of the paper.

Ziggy grabbed it triumphantly. "I found it, mon! Let the bells ring and the school day begin!"

The early bell seemed to hear him, for the signal to go into the building sounded just as he spoke. Ziggy stuffed the rest of his things back into his bag, tossed it over his shoulder, and called to Rico, who never ceased to be amazed at Ziggy, "Let's go, mon. We'll be late!"

Their school building was very old. It had five floors, with a large marble staircase leading from the front door on the main floor to the upper floors. The long, dark hallways were shiny with wax and worn by footsteps.

As Rico and Ziggy reached their lockers on the third floor, they saw Rashawn and Jerome sitting on the linoleum waiting for them.

"What's up?" asked Rashawn, yawning. He uncurled his long legs, stood up, and stretched. He had grown taller during the long summer vacation and was proud that his size-ten shoes were the biggest

of all his friends'. Lots of people said he looked like a basketball star. He liked that.

"Nothin' much," replied Rico. "Ziggy was having a homework attack, but he found it."

"So what else is new?" asked Jerome. "Ziggy loses his homework every day."

"It's not always my fault," replied Ziggy cheerfully. "Monday it was the jelly's fault, Tuesday it was my mum's fault, and Wednesday it was my new kitten's fault!"

"How do you figure?" asked Rico.

"It's simple, mon. Somehow, when I made my bologna and jelly sandwich on Monday, the jelly jumped up, landed on my math homework, and made my paper stick to the bottom of my book bag! The next day, my mum washed my favorite blue jeans with my science homework in the back pocket."

"I know you're gonna tell us," said Jerome with a grin, "but how did the kitten lose your homework?"

"She didn't lose it, mon—she attacked it!"

"What?"

"There's a reason I named that crazy kitten Jungle Kitty. She runs around the house acting like she's a lion or tiger, and attacking dangerous creatures like shoes and pieces of paper."

"What if she saw a mouse?" asked Rashawn.

"She'd probably run the other way, mon," Ziggy said, laughing. "But she really had fun beating up my homework paper that night!"

"Did Jungle Kitty get last night's history homework too?" Jerome asked.

"No way, mon. This one was too important. It tried to hide from me, but I knew where it was all the time. There's no way I'm gonna miss that field trip!"

Mrs. Powell, their teacher, was taking them on an all-day field trip to the Ohio River. Only the students who turned in their homework would be allowed to go, so Ziggy and the rest of the class had been extra careful to have it ready.

Jerome was shorter than Rashawn, but was strong and tough-looking. His face was brown and leathery, like the bomber jacket he wore every day.

He checked his book bag for his homework, and grinned at the other boys. "This is gonna be an awesome field trip—lunch on the riverbank and a boat ride!"

"You got that right," replied Rico. He was neatly dressed in dark blue pants and a light blue shirt. His coffee-colored, smiling face was surrounded by thick, curly brown hair. His book bag, unlike the other boys', was neat and organized. His history homework was always in his green history folder, and his math homework was always in his blue math folder. He liked to draw pictures of houses and kept those drawings in a special red folder—he said one day he'd like to be an architect.

Mrs. Powell came around the corner just as the bell rang to begin class, jiggling keys and balancing a coffee cup on a large stack of papers.

"Looks like I made it just in time," she called out cheerfully. "I was making last-minute plans for our trip," she explained as she unlocked the classroom door. "Now where did he go? He was right behind me."

"Who?" asked Jerome.

"Oh, there he is! Come on in, Mr. Greene. Welcome to our classroom."

Mr. Greene walked slowly around the corner. He was almost bald, with wisps of curly, gray hair, and golden copper, slightly wrinkled skin. His dark eyes twinkled as he saw Rico, Rashawn, Jerome, and Ziggy standing in the hallway, staring in surprise.

"Well, if it isn't the Black Dinosaurs!" said Mr. Greene with a chuckle. "Good to see you again!"

Two

"Hey, Mr. Greene! What are you doing here, mon?" asked Ziggy.

"Your teacher asked me to go along on your field trip today," replied Mr. Greene with a smile.

"Why would an old dude like you want to go on a trip with a bunch of kids?" Rico asked.

"Just wait and see," whispered Mr. Greene with mystery in his voice. "But tell me about you—have you had any meetings of the Black Dinosaurs lately?"

The Black Dinosaurs was the name of the club that Ziggy, Rashawn, Rico, and Jerome had started that past summer. They had built a clubhouse in

Ziggy's backyard, and Mr. Greene had helped them solve a mystery about a buried box of bones.

"Sure, mon," replied Ziggy, "but since school has started, we usually only meet on Saturday. Stop by sometime and see us. I'm bringing peanut butter pizza this week!"

Mr. Greene grabbed his throat, pretended to gag, and groaned, "No thanks—not this time."

Rico and Jerome giggled, and Rashawn whispered, "If Ziggy brings it, I'm gonna make him eat the whole thing!"

They walked into the classroom, talking and laughing, found their seats, and waited to find out why Mr. Greene was joining them on their field trip.

Mrs. Powell, who was dressed in jeans, a sweatshirt, and tennis shoes instead of her usual suit and black, patent leather heels, was in a good mood. She took attendance, collected the homework, and cheered when every single homework paper was turned in.

"Class, the bus is here. Be sure you have your

lunch with you. Let's go! Mr. Greene, it's right this way, sir."

They all trooped noisily down the stairs, while Mrs. Powell told them, "Hush! You'll disturb the other classes." Nobody really got any quieter, but at least she tried. Mrs. Powell checked names as each person got on the bus, and when everyone was seated, the bus roared away from the school while the kids inside cheered.

Ziggy was sitting next to Rico and right behind Mr. Greene and Mrs. Powell. "So what's going on, mon?" he whispered in Mr. Greene's ear.

"I like the river," replied Mr. Greene.

"You like it so much that you got on a school bus full of kids just to see it?" asked Rico. "You could have walked down to the river from your house."

"I often do, Rico," replied Mr. Greene. "Sometimes before daybreak I walk down here and watch the morning wake up and the day begin its business. It's a wonderful sight."

"Awesome, mon," replied Ziggy as he settled back into his seat.

The school was not very far from the river, so it wasn't long before the bus stopped at Eden Park and the kids got off the bus. The weather was a little chilly, but the bright sunlight made the day seem warm and cheerful. The trees had lost most of their leaves; they looked as if they might shiver when the warmth of the sun left for the night.

Ziggy and his classmates walked through the park a short way, then stopped at a low stone wall. Suddenly there was silence. Fifty feet below them, shining in the sunlight, was the Ohio River.

"Wow!" whispered Rashawn. "My mom and dad and I have driven over the bridge lots of times, but all you can really see from the car window is a little bit of dirty brown water. I never knew the river was so pretty!"

Silent and powerful, and filled with dark mysteries, the river relaxed at their feet. Like a long, purple serpent, it curled lazily as it wound its way from there to wherever. Although it was crossed by modern bridges and dotted with boats and barges, the river seemed strong, as if it were ignoring the dirt and pollution of the present and remembering the glory of its past.

"That's Kentucky, isn't it, Mrs. Powell?" asked Rico, pointing to the buildings across the river. "It seems like it's close enough to touch, but it also seems like it's a million miles away."

"You're right, Rico, and I know what you mean," Mrs. Powell agreed. "When we get on the boat this afternoon, you'll be able to see how far away and yet how close it really is."

Suddenly Ziggy pointed and cried out, "There's our boat! Look! It says '*BB Riverboat*'! They're loading up! We're gonna miss it, mon!"

"Calm down, Ziggy," replied Mrs. Powell patiently. "We don't have to be on our boat for another hour. They won't leave without us. I promise."

The children sat or stood near the wall, and the river seemed to quiet them as they listened to its silent story. "This is nice," said Jerome softly. "The wind is blowing, the sun is shining, and there's no bugs!"

"I bet if that old river could talk, he'd have some mighty stories to tell," Rico said thoughtfully.

"Is the water very deep?" asked Nicole, a girl with long black braids and a questioning look constantly on her face. Rico thought she looked confused. Jerome thought she looked cute. Ziggy hadn't noticed her at all.

"It sure is," replied Mr. Greene, "very deep and cold. And you're right, Rico. There are some really powerful stories from the river. That's why I'm here today."

"True stories?" asked Tiana, a tall, thin, toffee-tanned girl. She moved closer to Rashawn, who was the only boy in class taller than she was. Rashawn pretended he didn't notice and looked only at Mr. Greene.

"Oh, yes—very true," replied Mr. Greene. "My daddy and my granddaddy both grew up down here on the river. My granddaddy worked on the big riverboats that went from here all the way down the Mississippi River to New Orleans. And my daddy

worked on the docks, lifting and loading, all his life. From the time I was a very small boy, they told me stories from the river—tales of sailors and chases and losers and lovers."

At the word "lovers," Tiana edged one step closer to Rashawn. He pretended he had to sneeze and moved one step away.

"Tell us about some of the chases, mon!" cried Ziggy with excitement.

Rashawn quickly joined in. "Yeah! We want to hear some adventure stories!" The rest of the class loudly agreed. Tiana sighed and whispered to Nicole, "I'd rather hear some of the love stories." Nicole smiled and nodded her head.

"Did you know," asked Mr. Greene, "that the Ohio River was a major route of the Underground Railroad?"

"That's wacko, mon! I thought you said these were true stories!" argued Ziggy. "What kind of rail-road goes under the ground or under a river?"

"Don't you ever do your homework, Ziggy?"

sniffed Tiffany with a knowing look. "It was all about—"

"Slaves and stuff!" replied Ziggy. "I know because I did it while I was watching TV."

"If you had turned off the TV and read the last page, you would have come to the part about the Underground Railroad. Isn't that right, Mrs. Powell?" asked Tiffany, even though she was sure of the answer.

"She's right, Ziggy," Mrs. Powell replied with a smile. "The last part of your homework was to read those pages in the book on the Underground Railroad."

"Oh, no!" cried Ziggy, who smacked himself in the forehead as if he were really upset. "Did you say 'read' those pages? I thought you said 'reach' that part! So I reached it, and closed my book. Then I fixed myself a tomato and banana milkshake and went to bed, mon!"

Nobody believed Ziggy, but everyone laughed— even Mrs. Powell. Ziggy grinned, and Mr. Greene spoke softly. "I'm going to tell you a tale that you can't find in your history books, and it's a true story. Listen!"

The class gathered in a circle, sat on the grass and waited for Mr. Greene to begin.

Three

"The Underground Railroad," Mr. Greene began, "was not a railroad at all. It was a method used to help slaves escape from the South and get to the North, where they could be free. It was very dangerous, but it was daring and mysterious, too."

"So why was it called a railroad?" asked Rashawn.

"Let me explain. It was run like an invisible train. The escaped slaves had to travel long distances, and they made stops at safe houses—homes of people who helped them to the next location. Folks who didn't understand about the secret hiding places

would say that it seemed like the people just *disappeared underground*."

"Awesome, mon!" whispered Ziggy.

"Everything had to be kept secret because it was against the law for a slave to try to escape, and it was against the law for anyone to help a slave to escape," continued Mr. Greene.

Nicole was shocked. "You mean you'd go to jail for wanting to be free?" she asked.

"No, you wouldn't go to jail—if you were an escaped slave who was captured, you would go back to your owner and back to slavery, where you would probably be punished severely."

"They'd never catch me!" said Jerome with his head held high.

"Maybe not, Jerome, but many people were caught."

"How did they travel, Mr. Greene?" asked Nicole.

"Sometimes by wagon, but mostly they traveled on foot."

"You mean they *walked* from way down South to

way up North?" asked Jerome with amazement. "I rode in a car from Georgia to Ohio with my grandmother and my two loud little sisters, and it seemed to take forever!"

"Do you know anybody who walked here, Mr. Greene?" asked Mimi, a small, quiet girl sitting on the grass near Rico.

"I sure do, little one," replied Mr. Greene. "That's why your teacher asked me to come today. My granddaddy, Mac, came to Cincinnati on the Underground Railroad!"

"Well, don't just sit there, mon! Tell us the story!" Ziggy urged.

"When Mac was just a little older than you kids are, his mama decided to leave slavery in Georgia and try to get to freedom here in Cincinnati. She had heard her owner say that he was going to sell her, so she left that night with a small pack in one arm, her only son, Mac, holding on to the other, and a dream in her heart to be free."

"Selling people! That stinks!" Tiana cried indignantly.

"Yes," Mr. Greene said, smiling ruefully at Tiana's exclamation. "It certainly did stink. So she left. She walked slowly through the woods each night, following the North Star when the nights were clear, and looking for other signs—like moss on the trees and the direction of flowing streams—when clouds covered the night sky. She was afraid of the sounds and the darkness of the night, but she was more afraid of being captured and returned to slavery. She and Mac hid during the day and tried to sleep in the woods with leaves and branches over them. It was very hot and insect bites covered them."

"Bugs?" asked Jerome. "It must have been awful!"

Mr. Greene chuckled. "The bugs were nothing compared to the hunger. All they had to eat was berries from the woods. Just when they thought they could go no farther, a wagon appeared on the road. Mac was afraid they'd be captured, but the driver of the wagon was friendly. He took them to his house, where he fed them and hid them in a tunnel under his basement for three days."

"Underground! Now I get it!" said Rico.

"That courageous person took Mac and his mama to a farm where someone else hid them in a barn for a week. I think they must have hidden at several different homes. Each stop got them closer to the river. When they finally got to the Ohio River—"

"They got in a car and came across the bridge, mon!" finished Ziggy, giggling.

"Yeah, right," Mr. Greene replied with a smile. "None of these bridges had even been built yet. What really happened was, they were put in a packing box, addressed to a lady in Cincinnati, and put on a ferry boat to cross the river. The lady was here on the other side when they arrived, they were unpacked in Ohio, and were free!"

"Hooray!" the class cheered. "Mac and his mama were safe!"

"Not quite," said Mr. Greene, sighing. "They still had to hide for several weeks until they could get proper papers. If a slave catcher saw them, they could be forced to return to slavery."

"That's not fair!" several kids shouted at once.

"You're right," said Mr. Greene.

"So where did they hide?" Rico wanted to know.

"Well, there were many possibilities," answered Mr. Greene. "There were basements and attics and barns that were used as hiding places. Also, many of the houses built back then had secret rooms."

"Secret rooms?" asked Nicole.

"Here in Cincinnati?" Tiana wondered.

"How could a room be secret?" Jerome asked.

"Some rooms were hidden behind walls or under trapdoors," replied Mr. Greene. "They were very small. And some were just dirt tunnels that served as a means of escape from the house to the outside."

"So where did Mac and his mama hide?" asked Rico.

"They hid," Mr. Greene said dramatically, "in secret rooms that are located *right underneath your school*!" For a moment the children were silent with disbelief.

"What do you mean secret rooms under our school?" Jerome finally asked.

"Have you seen any of the secret rooms, Mr. Greene?" asked Rashawn.

"No, Rashawn, I haven't. But my daddy and my granddaddy Mac used to tell me stories about them. You see, an old farm that was a hiding place for the Underground Railroad used to stand where your school is now located. When your school was built almost a hundred years ago, the old tunnels and secret rooms were lost, but not forgotten."

"Is that true, Mrs. Powell?" asked Rico.

"Mr. Greene is the expert on this," replied Mrs. Powell. "I've always heard stories about the secret passageways hidden under our school, but I never really believed them . . . just like the story of the River City Ghost."

"*Ghost?* What ghost? Who is the River City Ghost?" The children fired questions at Mrs. Powell. Rico glanced at Ziggy and shivered.

"My grandmother used to tell me the story of the River City Ghost when I was just a little girl," replied Mrs. Powell. "I'm sure it's just something she made up to make us behave. But the tunnels and the Underground Railroad—those aren't make-believe. Those are real."

"So there really are tunnels under our school," Jerome remarked. "Amazing!"

"Yes, but they've been closed up and lost for more than a hundred years," reminded Mr. Greene.

"What about the ghost?" asked Rico. "Will you tell us the story that your grandmother told you, Mrs. Powell?"

"Maybe the River City Ghost lives in one of those lost tunnels, mon!" Ziggy suggested eagerly.

"It's strange that you should say that, Ziggy," replied Mrs. Powell. "There *is* a tunnel in the story. Maybe there's a connection!"

"Tell us the story, Mrs. Powell," Tiana pleaded. She shivered and moved closer to Rashawn.

"All right," agreed Mrs. Powell. "Listen, children!"

"Awesome, mon," said Ziggy eagerly. "Marvelous mysteries all around us!"

Four

"Late at night, after everyone had gone to bed," Mrs. Powell began, "a strange whistling wind could be heard, blowing from the river and over the streets of Cincinnati. Sometimes it sounded like a voice; sometimes it sounded like a song."

"Did you ever hear it?" asked Nicole.

"One night while I was sleeping in my grandma's big, soft feather bed, I heard it, or at least I thought I did."

"Were you scared?"

"No, because I was warm and safe in my grandma's bed. Then she heard that whispering wind too, so she told me the story."

With the wind from the river blowing gently about them, the children sat spellbound, listening to Mrs. Powell's tale. Mr. Greene, with a twinkle in his eye, smiled at the scene.

Mrs. Powell continued. "Long before there were bridges and highways, about the time that Mr. Greene's grandpa Mac and his mother came here, there lived an old Shawnee Indian woman down by the river. She was about a hundred years old and was very wise. All the river men knew her and looked out for her. They would bring her fish, or cloth, or pretty shells that they collected in their travels on the river. In turn she helped them if they got sick or if they needed a place to sleep.

"Many people said that she also helped escaped slaves, but no one knew for sure. Some said that a tunnel ran from her place by the river, all the way under the city; others said it just seemed that way because she moved so silently and quickly.

"But everyone knew about her songs. Her voice,

sometimes sounding like a bird, sometimes like the whispering wind itself, soothed and comforted all who heard it. Listening to her song made anyone smile. She would sit by the water's edge at sunset and sing. Long after dark, her songs filled the night."

"What was her name?" asked Mimi.

"They called her Sun Spirit," Mrs. Powell answered.

"That's a beautiful name," Mimi remarked.

"One night the songs were silent," continued Mrs. Powell. "The folks who lived by the river searched for the old woman, but they found only the ashes of an old campfire and seven small, smooth stones."

At the mention of the seven stones, Rico looked at Ziggy in amazement.

"You know, in some cultures the number seven means good luck," Mrs. Powell added.

"I told you!" Ziggy whispered to Rico in triumph.

"So is Sun Spirit the ghost?" asked Jerome.

"No one knows, Jerome," Mrs. Powell replied

softly. "But late at night, after everyone has gone to bed, that strange whistling wind can still be heard, blowing from the river and over the streets of Cincinnati. Sometimes it sounds like a voice; sometimes it sounds like a song," she said, finishing her story as she'd begun it.

The children shivered, even though the sun was warm and bright. "That was a good story," whispered Nicole.

Mrs. Powell stood up, looked at her watch, and announced, "It's about time to head for the boat, class. That's where we'll eat our lunch." Everyone stretched and walked slowly and quietly to the bus. Each child seemed to hold a little bit of the morning in his or her mind.

"Thanks, Mr. Greene," Mrs. Powell added. "Your knowledge about the past makes it all seem very real to us."

"It was my pleasure," Mr. Greene replied. "And thank you, Mrs. Powell, for your story as well. The children will help us keep the old stories alive. We must never forget the past."

"Rashawn took my lunch!" screamed Tiana. "He said he was going to throw it in the river!"

"Rashawn, unless you plan to swim in the river to get her lunch back, give Tiana her lunch and get on the bus!" called Mrs. Powell.

"I was just playing," Rashawn protested with a grin as he tossed Tiana her lunch bag. "I don't want her stinky old sandwich anyway!"

A short bus ride to the riverbank took the class to the boat launch.

"Ooh. Yuk!" Nicole complained as they boarded the boat. "I see a dead fish!"

"You'd be dead too, if you had to swim in that polluted water where the boat docks, mon," said Ziggy.

The captain of the brightly painted *BB Riverboat* smiled as each student stepped off the walkway and onto the boat. The boat was large enough to hold lots of people, but they had it to themselves this afternoon. There were tables set up for them to eat their lunches, and large open windows to view the river.

Jerome stood by the window, felt the soft river breeze, and smiled with satisfaction. "I should be a riverboat captain! This is the life!"

Mr. Greene laughed. "Lots of people love the river and have made their living here. Go for it!"

Jerome, Rico, Rashawn, and Ziggy sat at a table together and ate lunch. The captain cheerfully rattled off facts about the number of bridges and the depth of water while the boat chugged down the river. People from the shore waved as they passed by.

"Are we having a meeting of the Black Dinosaurs

this week?" Rico asked as he stared dreamily at the water.

"I think we should," said Jerome. "We missed last week because of all that rain."

"Sure, mon," said Ziggy. "Saturday morning—ten o'clock."

"Sounds good to me," added Rashawn.

Rico like to watch the sunlight dance on the ripples of the water. Jerome dreamed of fishing from the side of the boat. Ziggy hardly sat still, jumping up to see every new sight. Rashawn kept looking at Tiana, although he pretended to be looking for other boats on the river.

"I wonder if anybody tried to swim across the river to freedom," mused Mimi.

"Oh, yes, I'm sure some did," replied Mr. Greene. "And they had to swim at night, when it was dark and even more frightening."

"Wow, it sure is wide," observed Nicole.

"And terrifying!" added Mrs. Powell.

"Why do you think it's so scary, Mrs. P?" asked Rico.

"Because I can't swim!" she admitted with an embarrassed grin.

Everyone laughed, and soon the boat returned to the dock. The tired kids climbed onto the bus with smiles of satisfaction. The ride back to school was quiet.

As Mr. Greene got off the bus to go home, several kids called to him, "Thanks, Mr. Greene. Come back again sometime."

"I'll do that!" he replied. "But first I have to rest up from this trip. Young people have too much energy for these old bones! Pay attention to your teachers, you hear? 'Bye now!"

"Good-bye!"

Back in the classroom Ziggy glanced at the clock. "Fifteen minutes before time to go home! Now, that's my kind of school day, mon!"

Mrs. Powell had been in a good mood all day, but she still remembered to pass out homework.

Jerome groaned. "What a terrible end to a wonderful day."

"If you give it a chance, I think you'll like this

assignment," Mrs. Powell told Jerome and the rest of the class.

"What do we have to do?" asked Rashawn.

"You better give Ziggy two of those sheets, Mrs. Powell," teased Rico. "You know how he loses and forgets his homework!"

"You might be right, Rico." She laughed as she handed Ziggy two of the assignment sheets.

"It's never my fault, mon," Ziggy protested, trying to explain. But he took the two sheets anway.

Mrs. Powell smiled at Ziggy and said, "What I want you to do is write a story."

"A story? On what?" asked Nicole.

"I want you to call it 'From Slavery to Freedom: A Story of Escape.' I want you to make up a story about either a person who was trying to escape from slavery or a person who helped someone to escape," explained Mrs. Powell.

"You mean like Mr. Greene told us this morning?" asked Rico.

"Exactly!" replied Mrs. Powell. "But this time you're telling the story. Think about the river and think about the people in slavery. Then make up a story about escape."

"I think this is going to be fun," said Tiffany. "When do we have to turn it in?"

"Today is Thursday. Let's turn them in next Wednesday. If you like, you can read your story to the class.

"Don't forget now, Ziggy," Mrs. Powell gently reminded him. "No more excuses, okay?"

"When have I ever missed a homework?" Ziggy asked with fake innocence. The whole class groaned and laughed. At that, the bell rang, and the school day full of river memories came to an end.

Five

Saturday morning dawned cool and bright. Rico headed down the street toward Ziggy's house. "Hey, Rico!" shouted Jerome from across the street. "My grandma brought doughnuts for us!"

"Great! I'm starving. My mom quit buying doughnuts when she went on a diet. We have a house full of healthy food!"

They stopped in front of Rashawn's house. His dog, Afrika, slept on the front porch. He glanced at the boys, wagged his tail once, and went back to sleep. Rashawn hurried through his front door and tossed Afrika a dog biscuit as he jumped down the steps, two at a time. Afrika lifted his head, sniffed the biscuit, and seemed to ignore it, but he put his paw over it before he went back to sleep.

"Your dog is so lazy!" said Jerome.

"He's a retired police dog," explained Rashawn. "He spent his whole life chasing bad guys and finding missing people. He's like Mr. Greene—just sitting around and dreaming about the past. He's allowed to relax now."

Just then Ziggy yelled to them from the end of the driveway, standing at the edge of his backyard. "Hurry! Come back here! I have something to show you."

The three boys rushed across the street and followed Ziggy around the corner of his house, down a path, to their clubhouse hidden in the back corner of his huge, tree-filled backyard. Breathless and laughing, the boys glanced over to see Afrika, asleep in the front of the clubhouse.

"How did he get here before we did?" asked Jerome.

"He knew where we were headed. He just took

a shortcut," explained Rashawn proudly. "I told you he was a police dog. He's really smart."

"Yeah, when he's not asleep!" teased Rico.

"So what's the big surprise, Ziggy?" asked Jerome.

"I found a clue to a secret from the past, mon!" replied Ziggy excitedly.

"What secret?"

"A clue? To what?"

Ziggy said with mock seriousness, "We must first go inside and have an official meeting of the Black Dinosaurs. I say the password today is 'Mysterious'!"

Ziggy was always forgetting the official password, and the other three always had fun watching him try to remember it. "I bet he can't even remember his own password," Rashawn whispered to Rico and Jerome.

Rico opened the door of the clubhouse. As he entered, each boy touched the huge, black plastic dinosaur that was hanging inside. Dusty leaves covered the floor, and a slightly chilly breeze blew through the holes in the walls that served as windows.

"Looks like we need to sweep up a little," said Rashawn.

"Looks to me like we need to spray for bugs!" Jerome replied quickly. "It's been a while since we've been here and spiders may not know they're not welcome!"

"We can do all that in a few minutes, mon," cried Ziggy. "Let me show you what I have!"

Rico couldn't wait any longer. "Show us!" he pleaded.

"First, tell me the password," Ziggy demanded.

"That's easy," said Jerome. "It's 'Ghost.'"

Ziggy roared with pleasure. "Finally! Someone besides Ziggy forgot the password!"

"I know," Jerome said with a grin. "I was just messin' with you, Ziggy. Isn't the word 'Mustard'?"

"It's 'Mysterious,'" Rico called out cheerfully. "Now what do you have to show us?"

Ziggy pulled a folded sheet of paper from his back pocket. He slowly unfolded it, smoothed it out, and placed it on the card table that Jerome's grandmother had given them. "It's a map!" he whispered.

"A treasure map?" asked Jerome hopefully.

"No, mon, a map of secrets!" replied Ziggy mysteriously. He now had their full attention. The map on the table was hand drawn and looked very old. It had lines and what looked like doorways, and the words 'Destroy this map!' written on the bottom.

"Where did you get it?" asked Rashawn.

Ziggy took a deep breath and began. "I got it from Mr. Greene. He got it from his grandfather. It should have been destroyed long ago, because it could have meant death to anyone who was found with it."

"What is it a map of?" Rico wanted to know.

Ziggy paused dramatically. "It's a map of an Underground Railroad hiding place! Not only that—it's a map of the hiding places that are under our school!"

"Wow!" The rest of the boys were truly impressed.

"Why would Mr. Greene give such a special map to you?"

"He didn't give it to me, mon. He just loaned it to me because he thought it would help me get a good grade on my homework assignment. I was walking past his house yesterday while he was sitting on his porch, and we started talking, and he ended up digging this out of an old trunk. I have to give it back to him next week."

"So how is it going to help you do your homework?" asked Jerome.

"It's not gonna help at all, mon," replied Ziggy with a sly smile.

"Why not?"

"Because I can make up a story about an escaped slave out of my head, mon!"

"So what are you going to do with the map?" asked Rashawn.

"It's not what *I'm* going to do with it; it's what *we're* going to do," said Ziggy, the excitement building in his voice.

"What's your plan, Ziggy?" asked Rico, who was

beginning to see what Ziggy had in mind.

"We're going to follow this map and find the lost secret tunnel of the Underground Railroad that's hidden under our school!"

Six

"**How do you think we're gonna find a lost** tunnel? Those things have been hidden for over a hundred years!" Rico asked.

"You know those old stairs behind the stage that lead down to a brick wall, mon?" asked Ziggy.

"Sure," remembered Rashawn. "Last year when we were in the school play, we used to go down there and hide from the girls and scare them when they came looking for us."

"There's a trapdoor back there too. It's built into the floor at the bottom of the stairs. But it has boxes over it and a big lock on it," added Jerome. "I used to wonder why those stairs went nowhere and why a trapdoor was hidden in the floor."

"The lock is open, mon!" announced Ziggy.

"What? How do you know?"

"Yesterday I was carrying some boxes for Mr. Lyon. He told me to put them in that storage area behind the stairs. And I noticed that *the lock was open*! It looked like it had just fallen apart because it was old."

"Did you tell anyone?"

"Of course not, mon! But I didn't put that trapdoor and the hidden tunnels together until Mr. Greene gave me this map. I just *know* there's a connection, mon!"

"What's the plan?" asked Rashawn.

"Mr. Lyon is having tryouts for this year's school play on Monday. Tell your parents that you're staying for that."

"I don't want to be in the play," complained Rico.

"You're only gonna be there so we can check out that trapdoor," explained Jerome.

"Oh yeah! I get it! Good plan!"

"What should we bring?" asked Rashawn.

"Flashlights," suggested Rico, "with extra batteries!"

"Bug spray!" declared Jerome. "And some tools."

"Some rope and a couple of garbage bags," added Rashawn.

"And I'll bring the map and the Seven Special Stones of the Sun, mon!" cried Ziggy.

"I don't think there's much sun where we're going," Rico remarked to Ziggy.

"Then that's all the more reason why we need them, mon! We'll meet in the school auditorium for play tryouts. Don't forget your supplies! The Black Dinosaurs are on the path of another adventure!"

The school day on Monday seemed to pass in slow motion. A few students talked about the homework assignment. Tiffany Lawrence turned in her story early, typed and stapled. Ziggy, Rashawn, Rico, and Jerome had other things on their minds today. They met at lunch to make sure they had everything they needed.

"After tryouts, when no one is looking," Ziggy explained, "we'll see if we can get that trapdoor open. It shouldn't take long to just take a quick look and see what's down there, mon."

"Do you think it might be dangerous?" asked Rico, who tended to be cautious and more timid than the others.

"Not if we're very careful," explained Rashawn. "Besides, what could possibly happen in just a few minutes?"

Jerome agreed. The bell rang, calling them back to class, but the Black Dinosaurs eagerly waited for the bell signaling the end of the day.

When the students finally assembled in the auditorium for play tryouts, Mr. Lyon seemed pleased with the large turnout. "Read over your scripts, and be ready when I call your name," he announced. "Think about what part you'd like to play."

By the time Mr. Lyon got through all the tryouts, it was close to five o'clock and almost dark outside. Rico decided he wanted to be in the play after all and tried out for the part of a young doctor who saves the lives of millions of people. Jerome tried out for the part of a young preacher who led his people to freedom. Rashawn tried out for the part of a great warrior who conquered many nations. And Ziggy signed up to be stage manager. "I like to be in charge, mon," he said with a grin.

Mr. Lyon thanked everyone for trying out, then dismissed everyone so he could lock up the building. He never even noticed that Ziggy, Rashawn, Rico, and Jerome, instead of leaving the building and heading for the late bus, moved quickly and quietly to the stairs behind the stage.

One of the girls, however, did notice. Tiana started to say something, but she didn't want to get them in trouble. She figured Mr. Lyon would see them and chase them out of the building. Her mother arrived to pick her up, and Tiana, after one last look at the big old school building, jumped in her mom's car and went home.

Rico and Rashawn easily moved the boxes off the top of the trapdoor. It was very old and looked as if it had not been opened for many years. The lock, as Ziggy had said, was broken. Jerome quietly removed it and lifted the large iron handle on the trapdoor.

"Give me a hand!" he whispered to his friends.

Rashawn and Ziggy grabbed the handle too. "When I count to three—pull!" directed Rashawn.

"One—two—three—PULL!"

With a strange creaking noise, as if it were yawning, the old wooden trapdoor opened slowly.

"Awesome, mon!" Ziggy exclaimed.

"Sh-sh-sh!" Rico reminded him. "We've got to be quiet!"

"What now?" asked Rashawn.

"There are steps leading down," observed Rico nervously.

"To where?" asked Jerome.

"Let's find out!" cried Ziggy. His face showed his usual cheerful grin, but his voice seemed a little shaky.

They pulled their flashlights out of the backpacks they wore and slowly peeked over the edge. The stairs leading down were made of wood. The air was very dusty and dry, but cool.

Ziggy went first, carrying a small flashlight. He put his foot on the first step. It creaked, but held his weight. Then he tried another step. And another. And another. Soon they could hardly see him.

"Come on down," cried Ziggy. "I think it's a hallway or a tunnel or something. I need more light. It's perfectly safe, mon—I think!"

Rashawn went down next, followed by Jerome, and finally Rico, who really didn't want to, but didn't want his friends to tease him for being scared. At the bottom of the steps, with flashlights shining weakly, Rico and Jerome looked around.

They were in a small room. Boxes were stacked along the walls. Jerome looked closely at one of the boxes. "Look at the dates on these!" he said in amazement. The boxes read, SCHOOL RECORDS 1900–1909.

"This is no Underground Railroad tunnel," said Rashawn with disappointment. "It's just an old storage room for ancient school records. I bet no one

in the school even knows that this room exists."

Rico still looked nervous. "Let's get out of here before we get in trouble!"

"You're right, mon," agreed Ziggy. "Hey, look at this—an old rope. I bet it was used by some old cowboys in a rodeo."

"Were there cowboys in Ohio?" asked Rico, who was starting to relax now that they were getting ready to leave.

"There were cows, weren't there? And boys? So I guess there could have been cowboys, mon! Watch me do a rope trick!"

Rashawn glanced over at Ziggy. Just as he started to yell, "ZIGGY, DON'T!" Ziggy pulled the rope. The trapdoor slammed down with a loud and deafening *thud*. Except for the thin beams of their small flashlights, sudden darkness surrounded them.

Seven

Rico shrieked, **"I want to get out of here!**
Now!"** Ziggy gasped and dropped his flashlight.

Jerome was breathing hard, but he said, "Relax, dudes. We have flashlights. We just have to go back up the stairs and push the door open." He swept his light around the room and across the floor.

Ziggy exclaimed, "Here's my flashlight, mon! But it won't come on. I think it broke when I dropped it!"

Rashawn shook his flashlight, but he could not get that one to click on either. "I'll check my backpack. I packed extra flashlights in there," he said, trying to see in the dim light. Rico, even though his hands were sweaty with fear, used his light to find the spares and gave them to Rashawn and Ziggy.

"Now what?" Rico asked. "I'm scared."

"Let's get that door open and get out of here, mon! I'm with you." Even Ziggy had lost some of his usual good humor.

Jerome climbed the stairs and pushed. Nothing happened. "I need some help here," he called. Rico, then Rashawn, and finally Ziggy, all crowded on the narrow wooden steps, pushing with all their might. The door would not budge.

"Why won't it open?" asked Rico. He was starting to be really afraid. He didn't like closed-in places and he didn't want the other boys to know how scared he was.

"Do you think anyone could hear us if we yell?" asked Jerome.

"Probably not. We're behind the storage area of the stage. There's no reason for anyone to come back here. I bet everybody is already headed home," Rico replied nervously.

"But we should try to get someone's attention in

case anyone's still around!" said Rashawn. "Maybe Mr. Lyon will come back here to check the lights or something."

They pounded on the door and screamed. Nothing happened. Rico couldn't help it. He started to cry. "It's okay, mon," Ziggy said gently. "We'll get out of here. Don't worry." But even he sounded worried.

Rashawn finally said, "Maybe there's another way out of here. Let's go down that hall." They took their flashlights and book bags and slowly walked into the darkness. The walls were thick with dust and spiderwebs.

Rico, still sniffling, followed closely behind Rashawn.

Jerome complained, "These webs are getting all in my hair. I think I'm gonna scream! If you see a spider, just don't tell me, okay?"

Ziggy, trying very hard to find his lost sense of adventure, was too scared to crack a joke. At the end of the short hallway was a door. "Let's try it, mon. What have we got to lose?"

The door was unlocked. It opened into a small room, empty except for a broken chair. Near the floor on the far wall, a hole had been dug. It was about three feet high. "I think we should see where it leads," suggested Rashawn.

Rashawn crawled through first. The hole led to a tunnel made of hard-packed earth. "Should we try it? It looks really long. I can't see the end of it."

"Suppose there's monsters or rats or dead things?" asked Rico fearfully. "Or ghosts?"

"We'll just tell the monsters and ghosts to gobble up the rats and dead things, okay, mon?" Ziggy said, trying to cheer Rico.

"So how will that get rid of the monsters and ghosts?"

"I don't know, mon, but at least they won't be hungry!"

Rico smiled a little and said, "Let's go for it."

In single file, on their hands and knees, the Black Dinosaurs crawled through the dirt tunnel, their flashlights the only gleam in the darkness. They were frightened, dirty, and starting to get hungry.

They moved slowly, bumping each other and feeling the sides of the tunnel against their bodies.

"Isn't this ever gonna end?" moaned Rico. "I know we've been in here an hour or more!"

Finally Rashawn, who was in the lead, exclaimed, "We're coming to the end of the tunnel!"

"At last!" cheered Rico.

One by one they crawled into a large, earthen room. "Where are we?" asked Jerome.

"You know what, mon?" said Ziggy. "I think we really have found one of those secret hiding places from the Underground Railroad!"

The walls of the room were made of hard-packed dirt, as the tunnel had been. It was tall enough for the boys to stand up in, and big enough for the four of them to move around comfortably. It was very quiet and smelled of old wood and rich earth.

"I think you're right, Ziggy. Look at this!" cried Rashawn. He had found a small bundle of what at first looked like rags.

"What is it?" asked Rico, shining his flashlight in that direction.

Rashawn looked closely at the bundle. "It's not rags—it's a shirt of some kind. And look—I think this is a cooking pot!"

"This might have been a weapon," Ziggy said dramatically, holding up a rounded wooden stick.

"It looks like a slingshot. It was probably used to kill more rabbits than enemies," added Jerome.

"But an escaped slave would have had lots of very bad enemies, right, mon?" Ziggy insisted.

"Sure, Ziggy," agreed Jerome.

"Do you think this stuff belonged to a real escaped slave?" asked Rico.

"I think so," replied Jerome as he touched the bundle gently. "Look! What's this?" Tied in a smaller bundle were seven smooth stones.

"Awesome, mon," whispered Ziggy. "I bet these stones belonged to a kid like us. I wonder if his grandmother had told him stories about seven special stones, like mine did, or was this just all he had to play with."

"Either way, I hope they brought him good luck," Rico said thoughtfully.

"This is so cool!" said Ziggy, his fears momentarily forgotten. "We've found a real live tunnel of the Underground Railroad!"

"Do you think this stuff could have belonged to Mr. Greene's grandfather?" asked Rashawn.

"It's possible," Rico replied. "I don't feel so scared knowing that this stuff belonged to someone who's like a friend to us."

"Won't this be cool to tell Mr. Greene when we get out of here, mon?" suggested Ziggy.

"You mean *if* we get out of here," Rico said, his voice quavering.

"Think positive, mon!" Ziggy was still trying to remain cheerful. He then took his own seven stones from his book bag and placed them gently and carefully around the bundle. "These are for you, mon," he said quietly, "whoever you are."

"Just think," added Jerome, "escaped slaves slept here and hid here and worried if someone would find them."

Ziggy exclaimed suddenly, "Turn off all your flashlights!"

"Why? Are you crazy?"

"Just for a minute, mon! I want to see something."

"What do you think you're going to see in the dark?"

"Just do it. One—two—three—OFF!"

The darkness was sudden and total. It seemed to grab the boys and squeeze the breath from them. Rico covered his mouth to stifle a scream.

"This is what it was like!" whispered Ziggy. "When the escaped slaves were hiding here, this is the darkness that covered them, mon!"

"Wow," whispered Rico. "They were braver than I'll ever be! Let's turn the lights back on!"

The beams of the four flashlights seemed like bright sunshine after that breath-grabbing darkness. Each boy breathed a little easier.

"Where's that map, Ziggy?" asked Rashawn.

Ziggy dug down in his book bag and pulled out the old map. With the four flashlights shining on it, the map looked mysterious and seemed to glow in the darkness.

"I'm not sure where we are," said Jerome, pointing to a small square on the map, "but this looks like it might be the tunnel we just crawled through."

"Where's the way out?" asked Rico. "I want to go home!"

"According to this," said Rashawn, "there's one more tunnel—and if I'm looking at this right, it leads right down to the river!"

Eight

"The river?" asked Rico.

"If Mr. Greene was right," Jerome said thoughtfully, "the escaped slaves would have to hide again as soon as they crossed the river. It makes sense that a tunnel would run from the river to a safe house."

"Didn't Mrs. Powell talk about a tunnel in that ghost story?" asked Jerome.

"Don't start talking about ghosts," warned Rico. "I'm scared enough already!"

The light from Ziggy's flashlight suddenly flickered, and fluttered out. Rico gasped. The darkness seemed to get larger with only three small beams of light remaining. "Who brought extra batteries, mon?" Ziggy asked.

"I meant to, but I forgot."

"Me too."

"So did I."

"Well, we're down to three lights. Let's find that last tunnel and get out of here, mon!"

Rico, who felt the darkness more than the others, scrambled to his knees and started checking down near the floor for loose spots in the walls. "I found something!" he yelled suddenly.

Another earthen tunnel led from the room and waited for the boys to discover its mysteries. Ziggy took a deep breath and crawled in first this time. The others followed closely behind. No one spoke much. Even Ziggy was quiet.

The earth in this tunnel was loose and damp. It crumbled as they crawled. "Can you see anything ahead?" Rico asked Ziggy.

"No, just more darkness, mon."

Suddenly Ziggy screamed. Jerome, who was

right behind him, bumped into him and yelled, "What was that?"

"I think it was a rat, mon! It ran right past us!"

Rico whispered over and over, "I want to go home. I want to go home. I want to go home."

They continued slowly through the tunnel, the dirt becoming mud that squished through their fingers.

"I think I see a light ahead!" shouted Ziggy.

"Do you think it's a way out of here?" asked Rashawn.

"I'm scared," admitted Jerome. "Suppose there's no way out and we're stuck here forever!"

"Stop talking like that!" snapped Rico. "Ziggy, what do you see?"

"It can't be a streetlight, mon," Ziggy reasoned. "Maybe it's some kind of light that's used when the sewers are checked."

"If we're near the sewers by the river, we're close to a way out!" exclaimed Jerome.

"All right! Yes!" they all cheered. Ziggy was so relieved that he forgot that they were in a narrow

tunnel and tried to stand up. His head bumped the top of the tunnel and his outstretched hand knocked the side of the tunnel wall. Suddenly, with a thunderous roar, the wet dirt that had been holding the tunnel together for over a hundred years collapsed. Dirt and darkness covered the four trembling boys.

Rico, terrified of the darkness, cried, "Help! I can't see!"

Rashawn and Jerome coughed and screamed, reaching out, trying to find each other in the thick blackness.

Ziggy shook the dirt from his head and face and felt a flashlight under his foot. He reached for it and quickly turned it on. The thin beam of light flickered weakly. The four boys sat huddled together in a space just large enough to hold the four of them.

Mud and tears streaked their frightened faces. The tunnel they had just come through had completely collapsed behind them. It was now just a huge pile of muddy dirt. The tunnel ahead of them that led to the light they had seen earlier was also blocked with dirt and debris.

"There's no way out, mon," whispered Ziggy desperately. "We're trapped!"

"Is that another one of our flashlights?" asked Rico hopefully. A faint whisper of light filtered through the rocks and mud.

"No!" cried Rashawn. "That's the light we saw earlier! Let's see if we can dig through some of this dirt. Who brought the tools?"

"I did," replied Jerome.

"Good, get them out!"

"I can't."

"Why not?" asked Rico with rising fear.

"Because my book bag is under all that dirt and mud. I don't even know where to look."

They all sighed. "Let's just use our hands, mon," suggested Ziggy. "Maybe we can dig an opening big enough for one of us to get through."

They took turns digging with their hands, but were only able to make a small opening. They could see a faint light in the distance, but the hole was only big enough for a hand, not a boy, to fit through.

"Do you think anyone is looking for us?" asked Rico. "My mom is gonna be really worried when I don't get off the late bus. I always call her if I'm gonna be late."

"What time is it, anyway?"

"I don't know. Nobody has a watch."

"It's getting really late—it seems like we've been in here a *really* long time."

"I'm hungry!" complained Rico.

"Me too," agreed Rashawn. "Ziggy, what do you have in your book bag?"

"I'm not sure, mon. Not much. All I have are some broken pencils, a green tennis shoe, and . . . Wait! I forgot I had this—it's my sandwich from lunch!"

They all cheered as Ziggy carefully unwrapped his sandwich.

"What's that green, lumpy stuff?" asked Jerome, who wrinkled his nose.

"Oh, that's the broccoli," said Ziggy cheerfully.

"Broccoli?" jeered Rashawn. "On a sandwich?"

"Sure," Ziggy said with a grin. "Doesn't everybody eat broccoli and potato chip sandwiches?"

They groaned, and laughed in spite of themselves. Ziggy broke the sandwich into four pieces. It was surprisingly delicious.

"That's the best sandwich I ever had in my life!" exclaimed Rico as he licked his fingers.

"We gotta get out of here," said Jerome. "When Ziggy's food starts to taste good, we're in serious trouble."

Ziggy's mood brightened a bit as he had an idea. "Let's toss the rest of this stuff through the hole. Maybe someone will see it and find us."

"Yeah, in a million years!" said Rashawn with a sigh.

"It can't hurt," Rico said weakly. He was willing to try anything at this point.

Ziggy took the rest of the things from his book bag and silently tossed them through the hole—two paper clips, the broken flashlight, several broken pencils, last week's lunch menu— taking turns until everything was gone. The only thing left in Ziggy's book bag was his green tennis shoe. With a shrug, he tossed that, too.

"Why not, mon?"

"Where's the match to that shoe, Ziggy?" asked Rashawn.

"I think it's at your house, mon. I left it there that day we took our shoes off to play in the rain."

Suddenly the last flashlight flickered out, and the damp, wet darkness, like a shadowy monster, gobbled them up.

Nine

Rico started to scream again, but the dark-ness seemed to silence all sound. Their hearts beat wildly, and all four boys were close to tears.

"I can't stand this!" cried Rico. "I want to go home! I'm not 'shamed to admit I want my mama!"

"My granny's warm blankets sure would feel good right now," mused Jerome.

"I wonder if I'll ever see my mum again," mumbled Ziggy.

"I'm really scared," Rashawn admitted. "What if we never get out?"

No one had an answer. There was nothing more

to say. The boys sat silently in the darkness, listening to the silence and wishing they were safe at home. Time seemed to tiptoe.

Only their rapid breathing and faint sniffling could be heard at first. Then softly, slowly, faintly, they heard the sound of a pale whistling wind, almost like a song. They could feel no breeze, but they knew that the wind surrounded them, and it soothed them.

"What is it?" whispered Rico.

"It's just the wind," Rashawn said softly.

"There's no wind down here," Jerome reminded them. "No, it's like . . . a song or something," he added.

"I think it's the ghost, mon!" Ziggy breathed quietly. "It's Sun Spirit! She's tellin' us not to worry. We're gonna be okay."

"The ghost?" whispered Rico.

"I just have a feeling, mon," repeated Ziggy. "Can't you feel it too? It's the River City Ghost!"

Jerome looked at Rashawn; they felt it too. The four boys shivered a little, then grinned.

"Awesome, mon!" proclaimed Ziggy.

No one argued with Ziggy. The strange breeze seemed to lessen their fears and helped them relax. It was like a song that warmed them from the inside out. The four friends sat huddled together in the darkness, frightened, lost, but somehow not completely alone. They slept. They dreamed.

Rico dreamed of a large, white house with tall, graceful columns in the front. It was surrounded by graceful trees and was filled with lovely old furniture and decorations. From behind the house, sad songs could be heard. On the wide, white marble steps in the front of the house sat a small brown boy, crying. His mother walked toward him, wiped his tears and hugged him. She whispered softly, "Tonight . . . tonight . . ."

Rashawn dreamed of dogs that looked just like his dog—but these were huge and mean and chasing him. He was running through the woods, and he didn't have on any shoes. Rocks kept stabbing his feet and branches scratched his legs. His side hurt from running and his heart was beating fast. The sun was going down, and he knew he could hide in the darkness. He felt strong because his dad was holding his hand, running with him. He knew he would not fall. *Tonight,* he thought. *Tonight.*

Jerome dreamed of two little girls who looked just like his sisters. They were in the Ohio River and were trying to swim. A huge boat with a loud horn was moving swiftly through the dark water, getting nearer and nearer to the wet and frightened girls. He tried to reach them, but the water was deep and cold. His granny appeared from beneath the waves and floated nearby, smiling. She wasn't even wet. He heard his granny say, "We'll rescue them tonight . . . tonight."

Ziggy dreamed of birds. He was a huge golden eagle, flying in the sunlight, in the bright, clear air. He could see for miles, and his strong wings soared with freedom and pride. He did rolls and dives and laughed out loud as he flew upside-down just for fun. The earth and the air belonged to him, and he shouted to the sun, "Today! Today!"

Gradually the cold and the cramped conditions

awakened the four sleeping boys. Jerome wiggled his arm because he thought he felt a spider crawling on it. Rashawn's long legs felt like pretzels, and Rico really needed to go to the bathroom.

Suddenly Ziggy screamed. "What was that?" he gasped.

Fear grabbed the boys once again as they listened to a terrifying rumble in the distance. It was a grinding, growling noise that seemed ready to destroy them.

"What could that be?" Jerome wondered.

"It's the ghost!" yelled Rashawn. "It's gonna get us!"

"The ghost is not mean, mon. It's gotta be something else! Maybe it's a monster," added Ziggy nervously. "Monsters live underground, you know."

"What are we going to do?" asked Rico.

They could barely move in the small cavelike area that trapped them. They huddled together in the darkness, listening in fear.

From the other side of the small opening they had dug earlier, the terrifying sound grew louder and closer and more dangerous. It sounded like the growling and scraping of a very large animal.

"I bet it's a bear!" cried Rico.

"There are no bears in the sewer, Rico. I think it's a huge rat!" Jerome shot back at him.

"It's getting closer!" shouted Rashawn with terror.

Each boy trembled, too afraid of the darkness and the approaching animal to move, even to breathe.

The scraping and sniffing and growling sounds were just on the other side of the opening now. The terrified boys could smell the damp, animal odor of the creature's wet fur.

It scraped and dug furiously near the opening. The hole got larger. Large hunks of dirt fell away in a loud thudding crash, and the huge, wet, black animal bounded straight at the four boys.

They screamed.

It headed first for Rashawn. He could feel its hot breath approaching. Then it licked his face.

"It's Afrika!" Rashawn exclaimed with relief and happiness. "Where'd you come from, boy? How did you find us?"

"I knew we'd be rescued, mon!" Ziggy shouted joyfully. "I was never even worried!"

Rico was more honest. "I've never been so glad to see that big, old, stinky dog in my life! I'll never call him lazy again! I promise."

The dog ran from boy to boy, licking their dirty faces, and letting them hug him. He seemed to know that they were lost and needed to feel safe again.

Ziggy exclaimed with a bit of his usual cheerful attitude, "Rashawn, let's follow this wonderful dog of yours out of here, mon!"

The four boys quickly scrambled through the hole Afrika had dug and climbed down a steep hill. Afrika barked once or twice as he led them to what they could see was a sewer tunnel. He ran back and forth, making sure that each boy was following.

When they reached the sewer, they could hear voices coming from above. Rashawn's dad was saying, "I hear the dog barking!"

Rashawn cried out, "Dad! Dad! We're down here!"

His dad, with relief in his voice, shouted,

"Rashawn! Are you okay? Are the other boys with you?"

"Yes, Dad. We're all here, and we're fine now. Afrika found us and saved us!"

Then Rico's mom shouted through the small sewer opening. He could tell she had been crying. "Rico! Are you there? Are you okay, baby?"

Rico wasn't even embarrassed to let the other boys know his mom called him baby. He had never heard anything more wonderful in his life. "I'm fine, Mama. We're all okay, really!"

"Stand back, boys," boomed Rashawn's father. "Here comes the jackhammer. They're going to open the sewer entrance so you can get out. This will be noisy, but it will only take a few minutes."

The pounding sound of the jackhammer breaking the steel and concrete of the sewer pipe rattled the boys to their bones. The silence when it stopped was sudden.

"Ziggy? You down there, boy?" Ziggy's mom shouted with worry in her voice.

"Oh, my mum!" Ziggy cried with a whoop of

delight. He was the first to crawl out of the sewer and up into the street.

Jerome followed, with Rico and Rashawn right behind him. Jerome ran to his grandmother, hugged her with all his might, and finally broke down and cried. He even hugged his two little sisters.

The boys looked around in amazement at the crowd of people who stood cheering and clapping as they climbed out of the sewer. Rico's mother, Rashawn's parents, Jerome's grandmother, and Ziggy's parents and uncles all hugged the boys, the worry on their faces replaced by joy.

Rescue crews with large digging equipment, two fire trucks, several police cars, an ambulance, and a television news truck were assembled. Mr. Greene, Mr. Lyon, and Mrs. Powell stood together. Several students from their class at school were also there with their parents. Tiana smiled shyly at Rashawn. This time he smiled back.

Ten

Wrapped in blankets and sipping hot chocolate, the four friends sat in the back of an ambulance, a little overwhelmed by all the attention. Mr. Greene and Mrs. Powell walked over to the boys. On their faces was that look that grown-ups use when a kid is no longer in trouble—relieved, a little angry, but really glad that everybody is okay.

"What got into you fellas? Ziggy, if I thought you boys were going to try to follow that map, I never would have loaned it to you," scolded Mr. Greene.

"We were just going to look around a little, mon," explained Ziggy, speaking very fast. "Then the door got stuck and we couldn't get out, and we got scared, and we followed the map until the tunnel caved in!"

"How did you find us?" asked Rashawn.

"At first, when your parents started calling the school and your friends because the four of you weren't home yet, we had no idea where you might be," explained Mrs. Powell.

"Then Tiana told your parents that she saw the four of you go backstage, but she didn't remember seeing you come out. She thought that maybe you might be up to something."

"When Mrs. Powell called me to let me know that you boys were missing, I knew it had something to do with that map," added Mr. Greene.

"We unjammed the trapdoor and followed your path until we got to the cave-in," Mr. Lyon said with fear still in his voice. "That's when everyone got really worried and we called the police and rescue crews."

"We heard the ghost, Mrs. Powell," Rico said quietly. "She's real, and she lives down there. I think

she must have been a real comfort to the escaped slaves hiding in the darkness."

"Ghost?" Mrs. Powell replied with wonder. "That's just an old story from long ago. You probably just heard the wind."

The four boys looked at one another and smiled. They knew that the whistling song they had heard was more than just wind. They had been touched by a voice from the past.

"Did you find the bundle in the Underground Railroad hidden room?" asked Jerome with excitement.

"We sure did," replied Mrs. Powell. "You've stumbled across a secret that's been hidden for almost a hundred and fifty years! It's a very important, very valuable historical find."

"Wait till you read my story, Mrs. Powell," said Ziggy with a twinkle in his eye. "Now we *really* know what it's like to travel on the Underground Railroad."

"It's dark, and it's scary, and it's dangerous!" exclaimed Rashawn. "Whoever left that small bundle was a very brave person."

"Mr. Greene, do you think it might have belonged to your grandpa Mac?" asked Jerome.

"I doubt it, Jerome," replied Mr. Greene, "but I sure would like to think so."

"What's gonna happen to that stuff we found, mon?" Ziggy asked as he stirred his hot chocolate with the pickle his mom had brought for him.

"Let's call the National Underground Railroad Freedom Center right here in Cincinnati," suggested Mrs. Powell. "I'm sure your discoveries will receive a place of honor in a display there."

"That's cool, mon."

Rico said quietly, "I didn't think we would ever get out of there. How did you know where to find us on the other side?"

Rashawn's dad hugged his son once again and replied, "We knew that the tunnel probably ran down to the sewer lines and then down to the river. But we weren't sure where to look. Mr. Greene gave us a general idea, but it was Afrika who found you."

"He squeezed through a small opening in the sewer line and came back with one green tennis shoe," added Mr. Greene.

"My green shoe, mon!" shouted Ziggy with glee. "That was part of my secret rescue plan!"

"Afrika then went back and dug until he found you," explained Rashawn's dad. "He's a real hero."

"Where is Afrika?" asked Jerome. "We haven't seen him since he found us."

"Look, mon," said Ziggy with a laugh.

Curled up in the front seat of the ambulance, with a green tennis shoe under his paw, Afrika, ignoring all the noise and confusion, was fast asleep.

Eleven

Ziggy's Story

Seven Smooth Stones
by Ziggy Colwin

Traveling on the Underground Railroad was a really scary thing. A boy named Mac ran away from slavery with his mother. They wanted to be free, so they walked four hundred miles to Ohio. It took a long time because they could only move at night.

It was very dark and they heard sounds that made Mac want to cry, but he didn't. In the daytime slave catchers were looking for them, so they had to hide in the bushes or in barns of people who helped them. It was summertime so it was hot, and when bugs bit him, he couldn't even scratch. Even a sneeze was dangerous.

When Mac and his mum got to Cincinnati, they hid in a tunnel under a house. Mac didn't get to play very much. All he had was a slingshot and seven smooth stones. Mac was a brave boy who didn't know that he was going to be famous. But I know. I was there.

The End

STUDY GUIDE FOR

Ziggy and the Black Dinosaurs #2:
Lost in the Tunnel of Time

DISCUSSION TOPICS

CHAPTER 1

1. What time of year do you think the story takes place? What is the weather like? Give examples from the first page to support your answer.

2. Talk about what it feels like when it's time to go back to school in the fall. Discuss the good parts as well as the bad parts about going back to school.

3. Describe the contents of Ziggy's book bag. What does this tell you about Ziggy?

4. Describe the boys' school building. How is it similar to or different from your school?

5. Ziggy seems to have trouble with his homework. What kinds of problems is he having? What do you think about homework and why?

6. Explain why Ziggy says he keeps the seven stones. Do you think they really have special power?

7-8-9-10. If you read all of chapter one, you'll see a description of each boy. Write a description or draw a picture of Rico, Ziggy, Jerome, and Rashawn.

CHAPTER 2

1. Tell what is revealed about the club the boys call the Black Dinosaurs.
2. What can you tell about Mrs. Powell from her description?
3. Describe Eden Park.
4. The class is sitting on one side of the river. What is on the other side?
5. What do the children learn about the Underground Railroad?
6. Why does the story of a railroad that ran underground seem so unbelievable?
7. Describe the kinds of foods that Ziggy seems to like to eat.
8. Why are stories a good way to learn about history?
9. Describe what the Ohio River looks like on this day.
10. How do you know Ziggy has not finished his homework?

CHAPTER 3

1. What additional information do the children learn about the Underground Railroad?
2. Why would a slave want to escape?
3. What would happen to a slave who escaped?

4. What did the law say about helping escaped slaves?

5. What was the usual means of transportation for an escaping slave?

6. What does Mr. Greene reveal about his grandfather Mac?

7. How did Mac and his mother cross the Ohio River?

8. Where would an escaped slave have to hide?

9. Where were secret tunnels supposed to be hidden, according to Mr. Greene's story?

10. What does Ms. Powell tell them about the River City Ghost?

CHAPTER 4

1. What do you think the River City Ghost sounded like?

2. What do you think the River City Ghost looked like?

3. Find out what you can about the Shawnee people in Ohio.

4. What did people call the River City Ghost?

5. What do you think happened to the River City Ghost?

6. Compare how the river looks from the riverbank to how it looks from the boat.

7. If you have ever been on a boat ride, describe it. If not, describe what you think it would feel

like to be traveling on water instead of land.

8. Why does Mrs. Powell think it would be scary to swim across the river at night? Can you swim? What would be dangerous if you decided to swim at night?

9. Why are field trip days so much fun?

10. What is the homework that the teacher assigns?

CHAPTER 5

1. What do you think the boys' clubhouse looks like?

2. What would be fun about having your own clubhouse?

3. Who forgets the password this time? What is the password?

4. What does Ziggy bring to show the boys?

5. Where did he get it?

6. Why is the map special?

7. What does the map reveal about their school?

8. Why do you think the words "Destroy this map" were written on the bottom of it?

9. What is Ziggy's plan?

10. Make a prediction. What do you think will happen next?

CHAPTER 6

1. What has Ziggy discovered behind the stage at school?

2. What is a trapdoor?

3. What is Ziggy's plan?

4. What does each boy decide to bring the next day?

5. What could be dangerous about what they plan to do?

6. Who notices that the boys have stayed behind? Why is this important?

7. What does it sound like when the trapdoor is opened?

8. How do you think the boys feel as they climb down the ladder?

9. When they get to the bottom of the steps, what do they discover?

10. Make a prediction. What will happen when they try to go back up the steps after Ziggy pulls the trapdoor shut?

CHAPTER 7

1. Describe how each boy reacts when the door slams shut.

2. Why are they in a very dangerous situation?

3. Describe the tunnel they find.

4. Why does Ziggy think they've found an Underground Railroad tunnel?

5. What is in the bundle? Describe each item.

6. Why are the seven stones they find so special to Ziggy and the boys?

7. What do they imagine when they turn off their flashlights?

8. What do you think it would be like if you were a runaway hiding in the darkness?

9. What do the boys learn about the bravery of runaway slaves?

10. What does the map tell them about escape?

CHAPTER 8

1. What did Mrs. Powell say about a tunnel in her ghost story?

2. Why do you think the dirt is getting muddy and squishy?

3. What do you think is the source of the light the boys see?

4. What causes the cave-in?

5. How would you feel if this happened to you?

6. What do they find in Ziggy's book bag?

7. What is unusual about the food they discover and eat?

8. What do they do with the items they find in Ziggy's bag? Why?

9. Describe a time when you have been scared or alone.

10. What would you do if you were trapped with the boys?

CHAPTER 9

1. Each boy talks about his fears. What does each one mention?
2. Describe the wind they hear and feel.
3. Why do they think it is the River City Ghost? Why is the ghost not scary?
4. Describe Rico's dream. Why do you think he dreams that?
5. Describe Rashawn's dream. Why do you think he dreams that?
6. Describe Jerome's dream. Why do you think he dreams that?
7. Describe Ziggy's dream. Why do you think he dreams that?
8. What frightens the boys when they wake up? What do they think it is?
9. What item leads to their rescue?
10. Describe the rescue.

CHAPTER 10

1. How do the parents, teachers, and Mr. Greene react to the boys after they've been rescued?
2. How is Tiana important in their rescue?
3. What do the boys tell Mrs. Powell about the ghost?

4. Do you think she believes them? Why or why not?

5. What is important about the tunnel and the bundle the boys found?

6. Where do they decide to take the treasure?

7. Describe what Ziggy is eating. What does this tell you about him?

8. What do the four boys, and their teacher, learn about the Underground Railroad?

9. How does Afrika find them?

10. What is significant about the green tennis shoe?

CHAPTER 11

1. What does Ziggy learn about the importance of remembering the past?

2. Write a story just like Ziggy's. Use your own words and ideas.

ADDITIONAL ACTIVITIES:

Use the Internet, an encyclopedia, or books to find out more about the following:

A. INFORMATION TO EXPLORE AND DISCOVER:

1. The Underground Railroad

2. Slavery

3. The Ohio River

4. Slave States and Free States

5. The Civil War

6. The National Underground Railroad Freedom Center in Cincinnati, Ohio

7. Treasure maps

8. Ghost stories

9. Riverboats

10. Unusual but healthy foods to eat

B. JOBS TO EXPLORE:

1. Teacher

2. Private investigator

3. Explorer

4. Emergency rescue technician

5. Riverboat captain

6. Archeologist

7. Historian

8. Architect or builder

9. Museum director

10. Mapmaker

C. WRITING ACTIVITIES:

1. Draw a treasure map that leads to something you've hidden. See if your classmates can find it.

2. Write a story with you as the main character in which you explore a mystery or make a discovery.

3. Make up a ghost story. Draw a picture of your ghost.

4. Write a poem or story about being afraid.

5. Write a poem or story about friendship.

6. Write a mystery that includes clues. At the end of your story show how the clues are solved.

7. Write a newspaper story about how Ziggy and his friends get rescued.

9. Write a newspaper story about how Ziggy and his friends are honored for their discovery.

10. Write a poem or story about a river, or an ocean, or any large body of water.